Dinosaur Day

by
David Webb

Illustrated by Derry Dillon

First Published
January 04 in Great Britain by

PUBLISHING

© **David Webb 2004**

A CIP record for this work is available from the British Library

ISBN-10: 1-904374-67-0
ISBN-13: 978-1-904374-67-1

Typeset by Educational Printing Services Limited

 Educational Printing Services Limited

E-mail: enquiries@eprint.co.uk   Website: www.eprint.co.uk

Contents

Chapter 1
It's Dinosaur Day

Terri Timpson sat bolt upright in her bunk bed and announced, in an excited voice, 'It's Dinosaur Day!'

There was a tired groan from the bunk beneath. 'Terri, it's too early. Go back to sleep.'

1

Terri's younger brother, Sam, was in the class below her at school and he wasn't going on the trip to the museum to see *Dinosaur World*.

Sam was fed up of hearing about it. He had heard nothing else for the past two weeks.

'It's Dinosaur Day!' repeated Terri. 'Come on Sam, we've got to get up.' And she jumped down from the top bunk and pulled the cover off Sam's bed.

'I hate Dinosaur Day,' muttered Sam. 'I'll be glad when it's over!'

Terri's mum was getting the breakfast
ready in the kitchen when the door burst
open and Terri appeared, her hair standing
on end and her jumper on back to front.

Terri's dog, Rebel, looked scared stiff. He took one look at the girl and hid under the table.

'You know what day it is, don't you?' asked Terri, as she sat down ready for her breakfast.

'Of course I know what day it is,' replied Mum. 'It's Tuesday.'

'No, I don't mean that,' said Terri, looking worried. 'It's Dinosaur Day. You have remembered to make me some sandwiches, haven't you? Mrs Tucker is taking us to the City Museum to see the dinosaur exhibition. I can't wait. I've been looking forward to this for weeks.'

'Of course I've remembered,' said Mum. 'You've reminded me often enough. Your sandwiches are in the fridge.'

'She's a pain,' said Sam, entering the kitchen and stopping to give a loud yawn. 'She's not shut up about it.'

'I knew there must be something special,' said Mum, pouring out two cups of tea. 'It's not often Terri's up first for school.'

'And it's not fair,' continued Sam'. I don't see why our class can't go to the museum. I'm more interested in dinosaurs than she is anyway.'

'Your turn will come,' said Mum, as Rebel crept out from beneath the table, his tail firmly between his legs. 'You'll have to see if you can bring an old bone home for Rebel, Terri. He likes a nice bone to chew on.'

At the mention of the word 'bone' Rebel's ears pricked up and he looked much happier.

'I'll tell you what,' continued Mum, 'when you get home this evening you can tell us all about it, eh? You can tell us all about your Dinosaur Day.'

'Yes, I'll do that,' said Terri, looking pleased, and she tucked in to her bowl of cereal as her brother Sam scowled and sulked.

Chapter 2
On The Coach

Twenty-nine noisy children were sitting on the coach ready to set off on the short journey to the City Museum. Terri had managed to get one of the back seats, together with her friend Jamie.

Unfortunately, Wesley Burke had also got a back seat. Wesley was the most annoying boy in the class and he was already causing confusion.

'Mrs Tucker, my seat belt won't work,' complained Wesley. 'I've got it fastened but it's too loose.'

'Then tighten it up,' said Mrs Tucker, and she grabbed hold of the adjusting strap and pulled it forward.

Wesley gasped as the belt dug into him, so that he could hardly move in his seat.

'There, that seems much better,' said
Mrs Tucker, with a satisfied smile. 'Now
then, children, I want you all to listen to
me,' continued the teacher. 'Our coach
journey to the City Museum should take
about forty minutes. I want you all to be
very sensible. No one is to get out of their
seats and no eating sweets on the coach.
Are there any questions before we set off?'

Wesley's hand shot into the air.

'Yes, Wesley?' sighed Mrs Tucker.

'Please, Miss – my seat belt's too tight!'

The children had not been travelling for more than five minutes when Wesley shoved his hand into his jacket pocket and pulled out a bag of chocolate flavoured toffees.

Wesley unwrapped two and shoved them both into his mouth.

'Didn't you hear Mrs Tucker?' Terri reminded him. 'She said no sweets.'

'Can't do any harm,' mumbled Wesley. He could hardly speak; his mouth was so full. 'I love chocolate toffees,' he spluttered and then he leaned forward and put the sweet wrappings into Lisa Broom's hood.

Ten minutes later the bag was empty. Wesley had eaten the lot. The coach was travelling over a particularly bumpy section of road and Wesley was beginning to feel most peculiar.

'He's turning green,' observed Jamie, as chocolate dribbled from Wesley's mouth. 'He looks like an alien.'

'Tell Mrs Tucker,' urged Terri. 'He's going to throw up in Lisa's hood if we're not careful!'

Mrs Tucker was not pleased. Wesley was dragged to the front of the coach where he sat with a bucket on his knee for the rest of the journey.

Chapter 3
The City Museum

Eventually, the coach reached the City
Museum and the children filed off and
gathered in the entrance area. The museum
was a huge, stone building and the children's
voices echoed as they chattered in
excitement, waiting for instructions.

Terri spotted a poster advertising *Dinosaur World*. There was a huge, fierce looking creature in the centre of the poster, its mouth dripping with blood.

Jamie, who was an expert on dinosaurs, recognised it immediately.

'That's a Tyrannosaurus Rex,' he said, pointing at the poster, 'one of the most powerful of all the dinosaurs, and that's a Triceratops behind it. I recognise it from the three horns on its head. I've got a picture of one of those on my bedroom wall!'

'I'm very impressed,' said Mrs Tucker, who had overheard Jamie. 'I can see you're going to enjoy our visit.'

A thin looking man wearing an official badge approached Mrs Tucker and introduced himself.

'Hello,' he said, shaking the teacher's hand. 'I'm your guide for this morning. Gregson's the name – Gregson the guide.'

Mr Gregson looked most peculiar. He was so thin that all his clothes looked too big for him. Terri thought he looked like a chicken. His long, scrawny neck stuck out of his shirt and his head seemed to dart forward every time he spoke. Wesley Burke was just about to make a comment when Mrs Tucker got in first.

'Now then, children, gather round and listen to Mr Gregson. He's going to explain how we are going to work this morning.'

The children shuffled closer and Mr Gregson began.

'Good morning, children,' he said, head darting forward, beady eyes shifting from side to side. 'Firstly, I want you all to be very sensible this morning. Our World of Dinosaurs exhibition is in the main gallery. No one must wander into the Egyptian Gallery. We are only just setting up the display and there are some very valuable exhibits in there, including the wonderful *Stone of Methesda*. We are the very first museum in Great Britain to show the stone. It is priceless. Absolutely priceless.'

Mr Gregson waited for a reaction but the children looked totally unimpressed.

'Yes ... well, anyway,' continued the guide, as his neck seemed to stretch a little further out of his shirt, 'the Egyptian Gallery is closed. Do you understand?'

'Ye – es, Mr Gregson,' chorused the children.

'Splendid!' said the guide, and he rubbed his hands together. 'I'm going to give out some clipboards and some worksheets and I want you to work in twos. Follow the directions on the worksheets and you should learn a great deal about the World of Dinosaurs. You will see that there is a section at the bottom of your worksheet to make notes about anything that interests you. Do you want to add anything, Mrs Tucker?'

'It all sounds really exciting,' said the teacher, and turning to the children she said, 'are there any comments before we begin?'

Lisa Broom put her hand up and said, 'Please, Mrs Tucker, somebody's stuffed a load of sweet papers in my hood!'

Mrs Tucker glared at Wesley Burke as the children moved out of the entrance area and made their way towards the main gallery.

Terri and Jamie were at the back of the group and, as they passed through the large, wooden doors that led into Dinosaur World, something made Terri glance behind.

Two men wearing dark jackets were lingering in the entrance area, watching the children enter the main gallery.

The men didn't move or look away –
they just stood and stared.

Terri wasn't sure why – but there was
something about them that made her shiver.

Chapter 4
Dinosaur World

The main gallery was massive. The children gasped as they moved into it and caught their first glance of Dinosaur World. The room was quite dark and it really felt as though they had travelled back in time to when dinosaurs ruled the Earth.

There were moving models of dinosaurs, huge fearsome, scaly creatures that looked incredibly realistic. There were sound effects that made the children jump and huddle together in fear.

There were pictures and posters and video clips of dinosaurs. There were glass cases of exhibits and, right in the middle of the great gallery, there was a massive skeleton of a dinosaur, bigger than a bus and as long as Terri's classroom.

'That's a Tyrannosaurus Rex,' said Jamie, his eyes wide in wonder. 'One of the fiercest of all the dinosaurs. Look at the size of its head! Look at those teeth!'

'Right,' said Mrs Tucker, 'it's time to start work. I want you to get yourselves into twos and begin your worksheets. You can start anywhere in the gallery – but remember to be on your best behaviour. Any questions?'

'Please, Miss,' said Wesley Burke, waving his hand in the air, 'I need the toilet!'

Terri and Jamie wandered off into the depths of the gallery.

The exhibition was fantastic. Jamie already knew a lot about dinosaurs and so Terri was confident that they could complete their worksheets. Some of the names were very difficult to read but Jamie recognised them immediately.

'Right,' he said, pointing to the first question, 'we've got to find the model of the Stegosaurus, make a sketch of it and answer some questions underneath.'

'That should be easy. The Stegosaurus has a really small head and a sort of spiky back like a dragon.'

'I can see it!' shouted Terri, and she pointed across the gallery to where a large dinosaur was standing among some strange looking plants.

'That's the one,' agreed Jamie. 'Let's go and draw it, should we?'

Wesley Burke was already sitting on the floor in front of the Stegosaurus, doing his best to sketch the creature. It looked more like a dog than a dinosaur. He was on his own. Nobody had wanted to be his partner.

'Nice drawing,' said Terri, glancing

over Wesley's shoulder. It wasn't, really –

but she was trying to be kind.

'I don't see why we have to draw it at all,' grumbled Wesley. 'We've got a picture of one back at school. What's the point?'

'Did you know that the Stegosaurus was as big as an elephant,' said Jamie, reading from an information board, 'but its brain was only the size of a golf ball.'

'I know somebody with a brain half that size,' said Terri, staring directly at Wesley.

Mrs Tucker arrived at that moment to see what the children were doing and Wesley took his chance.

'I really need the toilet, Mrs Tucker. I'm going to burst. Please can I go to the loo?'

Wesley crossed his legs and grimaced at the teacher.

'Oh, I suppose you'd better,' agreed Mrs Tucker, reluctantly. 'The toilets are in the entrance area. Be sure to come straight back, mind you.'

'Can Terri and Jamie come with me, Miss? I'll get lost on my own!'

'Go on then,' sighed Mrs Tucker. 'Anything to keep you quiet!'

Terri pulled a face and Jamie frowned.

'Well, thanks very much,' complained Terri as Mrs Tucker walked off to talk to Lisa Broom. 'That's made my day, that has!' And the two children followed Wesley Burke out of the gallery, leaving the rest of the class to carry on with their worksheets.

Chapter 5
Suspicious Strangers

The entrance area was deserted except for
the two figures Terri had noticed earlier.
They were standing near the door to the
Egyptian Gallery, hands in pockets, glancing
around suspiciously.

Terri couldn't help but stare at them. Her eyes were drawn towards them. She sensed that something was wrong.

The taller of the two men noticed Terri's stare and he nudged his friend and glared back at the girl.

Terri looked away immediately.

'They're over here,' announced Wesley, in an excited voice. 'Brilliant! I've been dying for the loo!'

'I'll come with you,' said Jamie, and turning to Terri he said, 'back in a minute.'

Terri wandered across the entrance area towards a notice board. There was a poster advertising the Egyptian Exhibition.

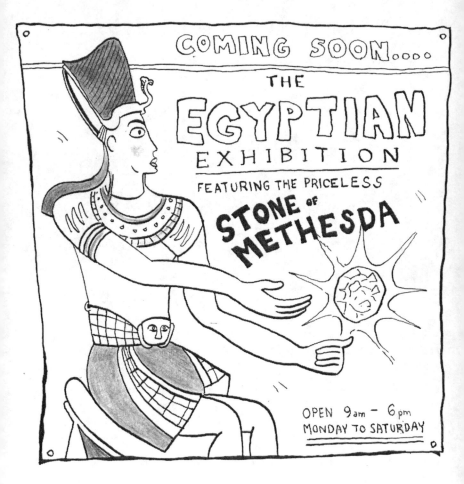

'Featuring the priceless *Stone of Methesda*' it boasted, and Terri wondered what was so great about an old stone.

As she stared at the poster, something made her think about the two strangers lurking near to the entrance of the Egyptian Gallery. She turned round to look at them and, as she did so, she saw the door to the gallery click shut and the two strangers had disappeared.

'I feel better for that,' said a familiar voice, and Terri turned to see Wesley standing there grinning at her, Jamie just behind him. 'Let's get back to the dinosaurs, should we?'

'Something doesn't feel right,' said Terri, and she glanced back towards the Egyptian Gallery.

'What do you mean?' enquired Wesley. 'Do you need a wee as well?'

'No, I don't!' snapped Terri. 'It's those two men who were standing in the entrance area before. I'm sure they're up to no good. I think they've gone into the Egyptian Gallery. I think they're after the *Stone of Methesda*.'

'Perhaps we should go and tell Mrs Tucker?' suggested Jamie, looking concerned, 'or Mr Gregson. Yes, let's tell Mr Gregson. He'll know what to do.'

'I've got a better idea,' said Terri, and the two boys stared at her.

They knew what was coming next.

'Let's follow them into the Egyptian Gallery. Let's see what they're up to.'

'Are you mad?' said Wesley, and his face turned pale at the thought. 'They could be criminals. They could be dangerous.'

'Well, we'll soon find out if we follow them, won't we?' said Jamie, and his eyes lit up with excitement.

'I ... I ... I need the toilet!' said Wesley. 'I'll meet you back out here, should I?'

'Oh, no you won't,' insisted Terri. 'You're coming with us!' And she grabbed hold of Wesley's arm and pulled him towards the door that led into the Egyptian gallery.

Chapter 6
The Mummy of Methesda

Inside, the gallery was cold and dark. The only light was from a small, square skylight set high in the gallery roof. It was lost in the great, gloomy room which seemed to stretch on forever into the distance.

'I don't like it,' whispered Wesley, as he stood with his back to the huge, wooden door. 'I've always been afraid of the dark. I really don't like it.'

'Shut up!' snapped Terri. Her voice was hushed and urgent. 'You're coming with us so just shut up!'

'I wish I'd gone to the loo on my own!' grumbled Wesley.

'I can't see a thing,' whispered Jamie. 'Are you sure they came in here? I can't hear anything, either.'

Terri listened. The great gallery was silent, eerily silent, as if it had been sleeping for centuries, as if it was waiting for a flood of light to awaken it.

Terri paused for a few moments and then she said, quietly, 'Let's move further in.'

The children crept forward slowly, carefully. Their footsteps made no sound on the cold, stone floor.

Wesley was shaking. He was worried that his teeth would start chattering.

Terri's eyes were beginning to adjust to the darkness and she could make out the display cases – huge glass boxes full of Egyptian exhibits. She crossed to the nearest one and peered through the glass front. It was full of pots and jars, stone dishes and different sized jugs.

'Wow! Look at this!' she whispered. 'Come and look in here!'

'So what?' said Wesley, peering over her shoulder. 'A load of old pots. So what?'

The next case was full of farming implements but Jamie had found something more interesting.

'Come over here!' he hissed, and his words seemed to echo in the great gallery. 'Look what I've found!'

Terri and Wesley walked over to a large, upright case. Inside was a huge face mask, the gold and blue colours shining through the gloom.

'It's fantastic,' whispered Terri. 'What is it?'

'It's a funeral mask,' said Jamie. 'The label says it's a funeral mask from the Tomb of Methesda.'

'Revolting!' said Wesley. 'You mean to say that's been in a tomb with a dead body? It's revolting!' And he turned away and wandered off towards another case.

A moment later there was a gasp of shock and Terri and Jamie spun round to see Wesley standing as still as a statue, staring straight ahead.

'What is it?' said Jamie, rushing over to the startled boy. 'What's the matter?'

Wesley didn't answer. His eyes were wide and Terri was sure his hair was standing on end. He raised a hand slowly and pointed directly ahead.

Terri followed the line of his finger to a long, glass case and, when she looked inside, there was an Egyptian mummy. It was completely wrapped in fading, yellowing bandages.

At the front of the case was a label that read:

'The Mummy of Methesda, 1450 B.C.'

'It's a mummy,' said Terri, turning to face Wesley. 'You've found an Egyptian mummy. What did you expect to find in an Egyptian exhibition?'

'Is it... is it... dead?' stammered Wesley, and he took a step backwards.

'Well of course it's dead,' snapped Terri. 'It's been dead for three and a half thousand years, hasn't it!'

'I don't like dead things,' continued Wesley. 'They're not healthy.'

'Don't be so stupid,' said Terri. She was running out of patience. 'You liked the dinosaurs and they were dead, weren't they?'

Terri stopped and raised a warning hand so that the others would not speak.

She was sure she had heard a noise – and it seemed to be coming from somewhere above her head!

Chapter 7
The Glass Case

The children peered upwards. A wide balcony ran around the edge of the gallery and it was clear that the noise was coming from there. There was somebody on the balcony and if they were not careful the children would be spotted.

Terri signalled for them to take cover and they crouched down behind the glass case containing the mummy.

'I don't like it!' whimpered Wesley. 'I really don't like it!'

'Shut up!' snapped Terri. 'Let's see what happens.'

The children looked on in amazement as the two thieves got to work. One of the men shone a powerful torch down onto a glass case, which was directly below the balcony. Terri noticed that two other thinner beams of laser light were also shining on the sides of the glass case and she guessed that they were security beams.

In the very centre of the case, sitting on a stand covered with black velvet, was the biggest jewel Terri had ever seen. It was the *Stone of Methesda*. Terri just knew it was – and it was enormous. It glinted and shone in the gleams of light and Terri could not take her eyes off it.

A moment later the strangest thing happened. Something made Terri glance back up towards the balcony and she let out a gasp of surprise.

One of the thieves had climbed over the balcony. He had a rope attached to him and he was beginning to lower himself down, slowly, steadily, ever so carefully. Terri could not believe her eyes.

There he was, dangling in mid air
above the display case, edging nearer to the
priceless *Stone of Methesda* with every
second.

Chapter 8
The Dangling Thief

'He's going to steal the *Stone of Methesda*,' whispered Terri. 'We've got to do something about it!'

'You're right!' hissed Jamie. 'We've got to do something about it!' He thought for a moment and then said, 'Any ideas, Terri?'

'We've got to raise the alarm. We've got to get help. If he cuts open the case from the top, the laser beam won't be broken. He'll get away with it.'

'I think I'm going to wet my pants!' moaned Wesley. 'I really don't like it!'

'You go back to Dinosaur World and get help,' snapped Terri. 'Be as quick as you can.'

'Brilliant!' said Wesley. 'I'd like to do that!' Terri shook her head as Wesley turned around and crawled away on all fours towards the exit.

'That's got rid of him,' said Jamie.

'We've got to break the security beam,' whispered Terri. 'We've got to raise the alarm before they get away with the stone.'

They edged forward in the darkness, moving silently from one display case to another, closing in on the cabinet that contained the fantastic *Stone of Methesda*.

The two thieves didn't notice a thing. They were too busy concentrating on their work, the one on the balcony holding the beam steady as his partner began to cut into the case containing the priceless stone.

Terri and Jamie were no more than three metres away. They crouched low and looked at each other.

'Ready?' asked Terri.

'I think so,' replied Jamie, his voice trembling with fear.

Suddenly, Terri leapt up and shouted at the top of her voice, 'Let's go! Let's go!'

She raced in front of the laser beam and a piercing alarm sounded immediately. She jumped up and down and pulled a face at the astonished thief who dangled from his rope in front of her.

Jamie joined her. He scratched his sides, leapt around and made noises like a monkey.

The dangling thief dropped his glasscutter and thrashed his arms and legs about wildly. He looked as if he was swimming out of water.

'George! Get me up!' he yelled. 'There's two mad kids down here!'

It was too late. George had dropped his torch and fled along the balcony, leaving his friend suspended in mid-air. The alarm screamed and the dangling thief screamed louder. It was absolute chaos.

'Leave him where he is!' yelled Terri, pointing towards the dangling thief. 'He's not going anywhere. Let's follow George.'

The two children raced towards the staircase that led up to the balcony. Terri spotted George edging his way around, desperately looking for a way out.

The main door to the gallery burst open and two security guards rushed forward. Wesley Burke was behind them, his eyes wide with excitement.

'Get me down!' shouted the dangling thief. 'Get me down from here!'

By now, Terri and Jamie had reached the top of the staircase and they were moving around the balcony towards George.

However, George had seen a way of escape. He had spotted a door and he was convinced that he could get away.

As the children looked on in dismay, he grabbed the handle, pulled the door open and disappeared from sight.

Chapter 9
Over The Edge

'Follow him!' screamed Terri. 'We've got to keep him in sight!'

The two children raced around the balcony and dashed through the door after George, the thief - and then they stopped in amazement as they realised that they had burst through into the Dinosaur Gallery.

There they were, looking down on
Dinosaur World, looking down at their
classmates and at Mrs Tucker and Mr
Gregson, the guide. But where was George?

Jamie was the first to spot him. He had worked his way around the gallery and was almost directly opposite. He was scowling and glaring threateningly at the two children who had wrecked his plans. The two security guards appeared through the door behind Terri and Jamie.

'He's over there!' yelled Terri, pointing across at George, the thief.

'You two stay here,' ordered one of the guards. 'We've got him now. He can't escape.'

As the children looked on, the two guards set off in different directions around the balcony. The thief was trapped.

They were closing in on him. There was no way of escape.

Below, in the main part of the gallery, Mrs Tucker and Mr Gregson had gathered the class together, alerted by the security alarm that still blared out its warning.

The onlookers realised that there was drama on the balcony and they stared upwards, mouths open, fingers pointing.

Wesley had joined them and he was pulling at Mrs Tucker's sleeve, trying to explain about the two thieves and the *Stone of Methesda*.

Terri and Jamie watched as the two security guards approached George. He was clearly trapped – but he would not be beaten. Suddenly, he swung his legs over the balcony rail and tottered on the very edge.

The crowd below gasped.

'Don't come any closer!' screamed George. 'I'll jump if you come any nearer!'

'Don't be stupid,' said one of the guards, and he glanced at his friend for support. 'It's all over. There's no way out.'

'I'm warning you!' yelled George. 'I'll jump!'

The guard took a step forward and then froze in horror as George launched himself from the balcony. The onlookers below gasped and screamed as he flew through the air. It was like watching a film in slow motion. And then Terri realised what was happening. George had leapt towards the great bony form of the Tyrannosaurus Rex, standing proudly on display in the middle of the gallery.

There was an almighty crash as he landed on the skeleton's back. The huge structure wobbled for a moment and then gave way under his weight.

Mr Gregson was horrified. He couldn't believe his eyes. He had stiffened like a statue. He looked on helplessly as George fell through the rib cage and crashed to the ground beneath, hundreds of bones raining down on him as he sat dazed on the gallery floor.

One final bone bounced off his head and the children let out a terrific cheer. They had never seen anything like it before. They had no idea that museums were such exciting places.

Chapter 10
The Journey Home

Half an hour later, the children were back on the coach. The two thieves had already been taken away and a very friendly police lady was explaining that she would need statements from Terri, Jamie and Wesley.

'No problem,' Wesley replied, proudly. 'I expect we'll be in the newspapers as well. They like stories about bravery, don't they?'

'Bravery?' repeated Terri, scornfully. She couldn't believe her ears. 'You were scared stiff. You were shaking like a jelly and you nearly wet your pants.'

'Anyway, have a good journey home,' said the police lady, as she left the coach. 'We'll be in touch soon.'

Wesley settled back into his seat as the coach roared into life. He had bought a huge bag of chocolate fudge from the museum shop and he was stuffing several large pieces into his mouth at once.

Terri and Jamie edged away from him. They were sure he was going to be sick.

'I can't believe it,' sighed Terri, sinking back into her seat. 'I was really looking forward to Dinosaur Day – but it didn't quite turn out the way I thought it would!'

'It certainly didn't,' agreed Jamie. 'We might have prevented the *Stone of Methesda* from being stolen but we couldn't stop the Tyrannosaurus Rex from being destroyed. Poor old Mr Gregson fainted when he saw it reduced to a pile of bones!'

Suddenly, there was an awful noise from the far end of the back seat.

Terri and Jamie turned to see Wesley
Burke leaning forward. His face had turned
a peculiar shade of green and he had a
handkerchief clutched to his mouth.

'Wesley Burke!' bellowed Mrs Tucker, as she stormed towards the back of the coach. 'I do hope you haven't been sick. I warned you not to eat on the coach!'

'No, Miss,' lied Wesley. 'I'm fine, honestly.'

Lisa Broom, who was sitting on the seat in front, was looking distressed.

'Mrs Tucker,' she moaned, and she edged a little further forward in her seat. 'I can feel something horrible in the hood of my coat!'

Also available from:

PUBLISHING

Chip McGraw *(Cowboy Mystery)*
Ian MacDonald ISBN 978 1 905637 08 9

Beastly Things in the Barn *(Humorous)*
Sandra Glover ISBN 978 1 904904 96 0
www.sandraglover.co.uk

Cracking Up *(Humorous)*
Sandra Glover ISBN 978 1 904904 86 1

The Owlers *(Adventure)*
Stephanie Baudet ISBN 978 1 904904 87 8

Eyeball Soup *(Science Fiction)*
Ian MacDonald ISBN 978 1 904904 59 5

The Curse of the Full Moon *(Mystery)*
Stephanie Baudet ISBN 978 1 904904 11 3

The Haunted Windmill *(Mystery)*
Margaret Nash ISBN 978 1 904904 22 9

Trevor's Trousers *(Humorous)*
David Webb ISBN 978 1 904904 19 9

Deadline *(Adventure)*
Sandra Glover ISBN 978 1 904904 30 4

The Library Ghost *(Mystery)*
David Webb ISBN 978 1 904374 66 4

Order online @ **www.eprint.co.uk**